YOU CHOOSE BOOKS

GOLDILOCKS
AND THE
THREE BEARS

AN INTERACTIVE FAIRY TALE ADVENTURE

by Eric Braun

illustrated by
Alex Lopez

CAPSTONE PRESS
a capstone imprint

You Choose Books are published by Capstone Press,
1710 Roe Crest Drive, North Mankato, Minnesota 56003
www.capstonepub.com

Library of Congress Cataloging-in-Publication Data
Braun, Eric, 1971–
  Goldilocks and the three bears : an interactive fairy tale adventure / by Eric Braun.
    pages cm — (You choose: fractured fairy tales)
  Summary: "A fractured fairy tale You Choose adventure about Goldilocks and the
Three Bears, featuring three different story lines and three different points of view"—
Provided by publisher.
  ISBN 978-1-4914-5855-6 (library binding)
  ISBN 978-1-4914-5928-7 (paperback)
  ISBN 978-1-4914-5940-9 (eBook PDF)
1. Plot-your-own stories. [1. Fairy tales. 2. Plot-your-own stories.] I. Title.
  PZ8.B6732Go 2015
  [Fic]—dc23   2015010248

Editorial Credits
Kristen Mohn, editor; Ted Williams, designer; Nathan Gassman, creative director;
Tori Abraham, production specialist

Image Credits
Shutterstock: solarbird, background

Printed in Canada.
032015   008825FRF15

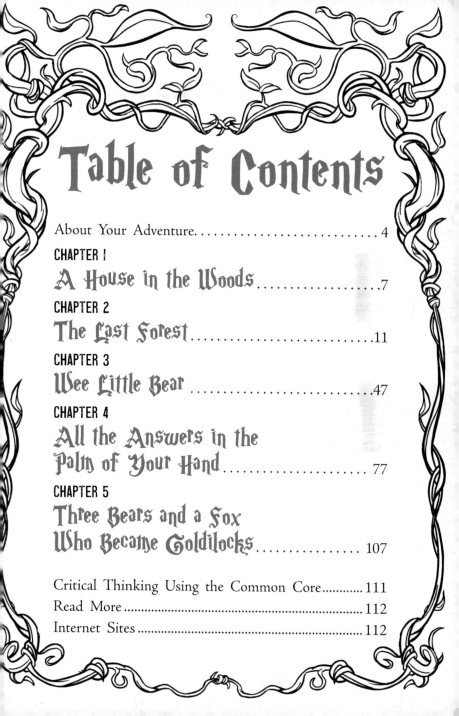

Table of Contents

The woods are alive with sounds. If you listen closely, they have stories to tell ...

In this fairy tale you control your fate. Assume the role of Goldilocks, or you can even try Wee Little Bear on for size, and make choices to determine what happens next in the story.

Chapter One sets the scene. Then you choose which path to read. Follow the directions at the bottom of the page as you read the stories. The decisions you make will change your outcome. After you finish one path, go back and read the others for new perspectives and more adventures ... and find the story that's "just right" for you.

A House in the Woods

YOU are walking in the woods. It's a beautiful summer day, and the sun shimmers in the canopy of leaves. A breeze rustles in the tops of the trees and makes a shushing sound, and a bright bird swoops toward you, then shoots away somewhere into the branches. A rabbit scurries through the underbrush, and you admire its cute puffy tail as it bounds out of sight. Water cascades over a rocky outcropping. You poke your toe into a patch of colorful mushrooms.

7

As you wander through the woods, you realize you're very hungry. You haven't eaten in a long time, and your stomach grumbles and twists. The longer you walk, the more you can think only about food.

The path you're walking along curves, then widens and opens up to a clearing. Before you is a little cottage. Curtains flutter in the windows. Smoke sputters from the chimney, but that's not smoke you smell. It's food!

The clearing is quiet except for the wind in the trees and a few chirping birds. As you walk up to the house, the wonderful smell grows stronger. You look in the window. Sitting at a kitchen table are three bowls—a big, huge bowl, a medium-sized bowl, and very small bowl. All three are full of porridge and letting off steam. Everything in the kitchen is neat and orderly.

The food looks and smells great, but you hesitate. Something tells you you're not alone.

TO BE AN EXPLORER OF THE LAST FOREST IN A WORLD THAT HAS BEEN TURNED INTO ONE BIG CITY, **TURN TO PAGE 11.**

TO BE THE WEE LITTLE BEAR THAT LIVES IN THE HOUSE, **TURN TO PAGE 47.**

TO BE A MODERN KID, NAVIGATING YOUR WAY WITH A SMARTPHONE, **TURN TO PAGE 77.**

CHAPTER 2

THE LAST FOREST

You wanted to see the real world, not "the World." That's what people call civilization now, the malls, skyscrapers, and parking lots that make up most of Earth's land. Even the deserts and tundras have been converted into one endless city. The sky is always gray from exhaust. Cars, high-speed trains, and hovercrafts dart everywhere.

There are laws against natural things. They are considered dirty and germy. Plastic and steel are easy to clean. How would you go about cleaning a tree? You've never seen one. Even your teddy bear is plastic, though not very cuddly.

You've never known a time before the World was like this, but your mom used to read you a fairy tale called "The Last Forest." It was about a place where flowers grew, insects buzzed in the air, and kids climbed trees. Sometimes your mother wept, she missed it so much.

Your mom died at age 30 from a lung disease caused by pollution. Among the things she left behind was a map. You'd heard rumors that there really was a Last Forest out there somewhere. The map seemed to indicate that it was true.

So one day you ride the subway out of your neighborhood and transfer to Lightning Train. At the end of the line, you hover-scooter past a garbage district and a graveyard for train parts.

Eventually you reach a great brick wall. According to your mom's map, the Last Forest is on the other side.

You hover along the wall until you find some loose, crumbling bricks. You pry them out with a steel rod you find and crawl through.

On the other side you recognize what must be a meadow. Your mother's stories described it perfectly. You never imagined that grass would feel so soft! And those tall brown and green things must be trees! Something smells sweet— flowers? You rub fluffy leaves against your cheek. Birds chirp. The sky is a brilliant blue. You think you may never return to the World.

When you find a cottage in the clearing, a delicious smell wafts out the windows. In the World, people don't eat real food—only nutrient pills. You've got to try whatever smells so good. You knock, but nobody answers.

13

TO GO INSIDE AND EAT THE FOOD, **TURN TO PAGE 14.**

TO WAIT OUTSIDE FOR THE COTTAGE OWNER, **TURN TO PAGE 16.**

The food smells so good—so real! How can you resist? You step inside and follow your nose to the table where you see three bowls. *Porridge!* you think. Something else your mother described. You're hungry enough to eat the biggest bowlful—but when you put the spoon in your mouth, you burn your tongue.

"Ouch!" you say.

You try the medium bowl, but it's too cold. *Strange*, you think. Then you try the smallest bowl and you find that it's just right. It tastes even better than it smells—rich and smooth and sweet. You gobble down every bite.

When you're done, you look around. The furniture is made of real wood, just like it was in your mom's book. A real fire burns in a real fireplace—something else you've never seen but have read about. You sit in the small chair near the fire to relax. The food in your stomach makes you sleepy.

Suddenly you hear a cracking sound beneath you, and the chair slumps to the side. It cracks again and then totally collapses. You're lying on the floor on the broken chair parts when you hear voices outside the door.

Your first thought is to hide. Who knows if they're friendly? But you are curious to meet these Last Forest survivors.

15

TO HIDE, **TURN TO PAGE 18.**

TO MEET THEM AND FIND OUT WHO THEY ARE, **TURN TO PAGE 20.**

Real food was tempting, but if someone actually lives here in the Last Forest, you want to start off as friends. Breaking into their house and stealing their food would not be a good way to do that.

So you sit on the step and wait. Soon three men come into the clearing. One of them is tall and muscular, with a mustache and hairy arms. One is short and stocky, as small as a kid. The third is somewhere in between. When they see you, the small one says, "There's another one!"

"Let's get him," grumbles the medium one.

"With pleasure," says the big one.

You didn't know that people in the Last Forest would be so angry! All you're doing is sitting on their front step! You consider running away, but they know the woods better than you. And you certainly can't fight them. You'll have to try to talk your way out of this mess.

TO TELL THEM YOU ESCAPED FROM THE WORLD,
TURN TO PAGE 22.

TO START CRYING AND BEG THEM NOT TO HURT YOU,
TURN TO PAGE 23.

You don't want to risk it. You run upstairs and see three beds but can't decide which would be just right to hide in. Gruff voices fill the hall below you.

"Hey!" says a deep voice. "Somebody's been eating my porridge."

"Yeah," says a slightly less-deep voice, "mine too."

A higher, scratchy voice chimes in: "Someone's been eating my porridge, too—and it's all gone!"

"Someone wrecked the chair!" says the deep voice. Footsteps bang on the stairs, and you dive under the smallest bed. What appear to be at least size 16 feet stop in front of you. To make things worse, the owner of this bed hasn't dusted in years.

"Achooo!" You couldn't hold it in any longer.

Size 16 reaches under the bed and grabs you by the ankle, dragging you through the dust and out into the bright room.

"What do we have here?" the big guy booms.

You squint at three men: a big guy with a fur hat, a medium-sized guy built like a wrestler, and a small fellow who looks almost like a child … but a mean one. They stare at you. You sneeze again.

"Another corporate scout from the World, I suppose," the medium one says. "Probably planning to clear away our last trees to make room for a plastic factory."

"I'm not a … a corporate scout!" you stammer, confused. But what should you tell them?

TO ADMIT THAT YOU'RE FROM THE WORLD,
TURN TO PAGE 26.

TO LIE AND TELL THEM YOU LIVE IN THE WOODS,
TURN TO PAGE 28.

Three men walk in the door—first a tall, heavy man with big, hairy arms, then an average-sized man with above-average muscles. A small, tough-looking fellow walks in last.

"Do you guys live here?" you ask.

"Obviously," the little guy says. The big one grunts. The medium one just stares.

"Are you from the World?" you ask.

"We'll do the asking since you're in our house," the little one barks. He seems to be the leader.

"Fair enough," you say. You tell them your name and explain that you escaped from the World to find nature. They get big smiles and congratulate you on escaping. They introduce themselves as the Bayer brothers—Big-ole Bayer, Medium Bayer, and Wee Little Bayer.

The Bayers tell you that they escaped the World years ago. Then the brothers tell you their plan: They're going into the World tonight to plant seeds.

Wee Little says, "We plan to bring nature back to the World, little by little. If people start to notice it, they might demand more. It's the only way to change things."

"Sounds dangerous," you say, thinking about the risks of bringing dirt into the World.

"It is," Wee Little says. "If we get caught, we go to prison. We'll never see the Last Forest again. Of course if we don't do something, they'll destroy the Last Forest. And then we'll be in a different sort of prison—a world without the Forest."

You want to help, but you're also afraid.

TO HELP THEM, TURN TO PAGE 31.

TO STAY IN THE FOREST AND PLAY IT SAFE, TURN TO PAGE 33.

"I'm from the World but I really wanted to get away," you say. "I want to live in the Forest."

The three men look at you in silence. Then the short one speaks. "You're not one of those corporate scouts surveying for the bulldozers?"

"No," you say, "What bulldozers?"

He spits on the ground then looks around and whispers, "People from the World are coming to destroy the Last Forest." Then the men introduce themselves as the three Bayer brothers: Big-ole Bayer, Medium Bayer, and Wee Little Bayer. Big-ole recently fought with one of the corporate scouts and scared him off—but the scout dropped a pamphlet. Wee Little pulls it from his pocket. It shows a factory that makes plastic plants for decoration.

Suddenly you hear a mechanical droning.

TURN TO PAGE 35.

You drop to the ground and start crying. "Please don't hurt me!" you sob. "I'm harmless!"

The little guy shakes his head. "I thought you were one of those corporate scouts, but you're obviously too wimpy."

He invites you inside. Over a delicious porridge dinner he tells you about the corporate scouts who have been sneaking around the Forest. "They plan to build factories here," he says. "We plan to fight them."

The brothers invite you stay and help them fight, but in the meantime you have to help with chores. After dinner you split logs and stack them by the back door. At first the brothers say you're splitting the logs too big. Then they tell you you're splitting them too small. You sigh.

23

TURN THE PAGE.

When you finish, your shoulders ache, and you have blisters all over your trembling hands. You never did such hard work in the World—everything there is automated. In the last hours of sunlight, you and the brothers pull weeds, bake bread, and patch clothes. But they claim everything you do is too fast or too slow, too little or too much, too soft, too hard. Is nothing just right for them?

That night you lay exhausted in bed by the window. A quarter moon hangs in the sky like the hook of a question mark. It's beautiful here, but you don't know how much more of this work you can handle. On the horizon the calm, easy lights of the World glow. You fall asleep thinking about your old life.

The brothers wake you before dawn. It's time to check the fishing nets down at the lake.

It pushes you over the edge. "Actually," you say, "Thanks for everything, but I'm going home."

The brothers look at you with disgust. You feel ashamed and you know your mom would be disappointed. But you're not cut out for this. You walk back to the hole you came through, back to the World, where everything's easy.

25

THE END

TO FOLLOW ANOTHER PATH, TURN TO PAGE 9.

"Yes," you admit nervously. "I'm from the World. But I'm not a 'corporate scout,' or whatever. I hate it there so I escaped."

The little guy snarls, "We don't appreciate people breaking into our house during times like this."

"Times like what?" you ask.

"A corporation from the World is planning to bulldoze a big section of the Last Forest to build a plastics factory. We intend to protect it—at all costs."

"Let me help you!" you plead. "I hate plastic!" You think miserably of your hard teddy bear.

The big guy crosses his arms and looks at you suspiciously.

The medium one says, "Prove that you want to help us, and that you're not a corporate scout. Or else." He cracks his meaty knuckles.

All you have is your mom's map, but you're not sure that will be of any help. Maybe you should try to escape out that open window.

TO SHOW THEM YOUR MOM'S MAP, **TURN TO PAGE 38.**

TO RUN FOR THE WINDOW, **TURN TO PAGE 40.**

"No, I'm not from the World!" you say in a panic. "I'm from … around here. I live off the land and stuff!"

"And off other people's porridge, I guess," says the wee little guy. "Where's your knife? You're just wandering in the woods in your fashionable World clothes with no knife?" The three men wear mostly furs and skins and carry knives on their belts.

"It's at home," you say, rubbing dirt on your shirt to make it look older.

"Quiz time," says the little guy. "What's your favorite flower?"

"Oh, that's easy," you say, thinking back to your mother's stories. "The bumblebee."

The three men laugh. The little one sneers at you. "Bumblebees are insects."

"I have a cat!" you say, desperate to show your knowledge of nature.

"Ooo, a cat," the big one says, cracking up.

"You're a real pioneer," the little one says sarcastically. "Hey, we could use a cat around here to catch the mice. One lives in a cave down that path on the left. Bring it to us, and we'll let bygones be bygones."

"Okay," you agree. You have seen cats before—they're cute and harmless. But as you approach the cave, you notice bones lying around in the grass. You get down on your knees and call into the opening, "Here, kitty, kitty!" A pair of yellow eyes looks at you, and you hear a low growl. You can just make out a black tail swishing in the air. Then you see its muscular shoulders as it crouches, ready to pounce.

29

TURN THE PAGE.

Suddenly you remember a word in the old encyclopedia your mom had. "Panther," you say out loud. It's the last word you ever speak.

THE END

TO FOLLOW ANOTHER PATH, TURN TO PAGE 9.

"I want to help," you say, deciding to be brave. "All my life I've wanted to change the World—to bring nature back. Let me come with you."

The brothers agree, and as soon as it gets dark, you're off. Deep in a dark part of the Forest, Big-ole rolls aside a boulder to reveal a tunnel. You crawl in.

The tight, moldy tunnel eventually connects with a bigger sewer tunnel. Soon you emerge from a manhole in a concrete alley. You walk to a government plaza full of statues of robots typing on computers. Medium pulls out his seed sack and a flask of water. He plants a couple seeds in a little depression on top of one of the computer statues. Looking into the depression, you are shocked to see that some soil is already there.

31

TURN THE PAGE.

Quickly you spread seeds in other beds of soil throughout the area—in roof gutters, trash piles, rain barrels, and empty coffee cups in trash cans. After several hours, exhausted and proud, you make your way back to the alley. But then a flashlight shines in your eyes, and you can't see. "Hold it!" a man yells.

You all freeze. Wee Little whispers, "Let's split up. He can't catch all of us."

TO GO WITH BIG-OLE BAYER, WHO YOU KNOW IS STRONG, TURN TO PAGE 41.

TO GO WITH WEE LITTLE, WHO YOU KNOW IS FAST, TURN TO PAGE 43.

"I'm sorry," you say. "I wish I could help."

Wee Little spits on the ground. You can tell he's disgusted with you. "Suit yourself," he says. "Come on, boys." He and his brothers head inside the house to make their plan for the night.

You feel bad knowing what they're up against. How can three Bayers fight the World? You know you don't have long in the Forest, but you want to enjoy it while you can. You head deeper into the woods and look for something to eat. You find some lettuce, but it's too bitter. Then you pick a few berries, but they're too sweet. Finally, you find an apple tree, whose apples are just right.

33

TURN THE PAGE.

Then as the sun sets, you look for a comfy spot to sit and eat. You find an old stump, but it's too hard. Then you find a patch of moss to sit on, but it's too squishy. Your third try is something soft and furry and warm. You settle in, but just as you bite into your apple, your seat rumbles. Then it growls. You look down to see a large bear looking up at you in annoyance.

You drop your apple and run as fast you can back to the World. Somehow that seems "just right" to you right about now.

THE END

TO FOLLOW ANOTHER PATH, TURN TO PAGE 9.

"Let's go get 'em!" you say.

Big-ole Bayer grins and gives you a heavy pat on the back that almost knocks you down. Wee Little rubs his hands together. "All right!" he says. "Let's do this."

You gather supplies and soon you're marching along the path, heading toward the bulldozer sounds. Eventually you see the exhaust from their engines puffing into the air.

"No guards," Medium Bayer says.

There are two bulldozers. Wee Little climbs a tree, and as one of the machines comes near, he leaps down and kicks the driver to the ground. He pops open the hood and you and Medium destroy the engine with hammers and crowbars.

TURN THE PAGE.

Big-ole Bayer climbs into the other bulldozer with the surprising grace of a panther and tosses the driver to the ground. He wheels the tractor around and you all climb on board. Big-ole cranks up the engine and plows full-speed through the brick wall. You can almost see the pollen and seeds and pure rainwater flowing from the Forest back into the World. Your heart fills with hope.

That night you celebrate your success, but the next day when you check the wall, you find that it has been repaired as good as new. Four new bulldozers sit ready to continue the work of the World. But you and the three Bayers are ready too. You will never give up your mother's dream of bringing back nature.

THE END

TO FOLLOW ANOTHER PATH, TURN TO PAGE 9.

37

You reach into your pocket, pull out the wrinkled old map, and smooth it out on the floor. "I do have this," you say.

The brothers gather around and look. After a few seconds of silence, the little one says, "Where did you get this?"

"It was my mom's."

"Your mom was the great Goldilocks?"

"Well, she was blond ..." you say. You describe your mother and they get very excited. "That's her! Goldilocks is a brave fighter," the little guy says. "She is a leader in an underground group known as the People's Last Forest Defense Front."

"Was," you correct them. You tell them that your mother has died, and the men grow quiet. They invite you to live with them, and they treat you like another brother. You meet others from the World who are a part of the Front. You join their fight to protect the Last Forest. You sabotage trucks that come in trying to destroy trees. You go on missions into the World to plant trees and bushes. You are proud to be able to give so much to a cause you believe in—a cause your mother loved.

THE END

TO FOLLOW ANOTHER PATH, TURN TO PAGE 9.

You take a small step toward the open window, and then you run. The big guy chases, but you dive headfirst and tumble through the air to the ground.

Wham!

When you awaken, your whole body burns with pain—especially your right arm, which is bent at an ugly angle. Blood from some wound flows into your eyes. The three men stand around you looking down. The little one shakes his head as the big one comes toward you.

"I knew he was a corporate agent," the little one says as they drag you into the woods. You don't know what they'll do to you, but you know it won't be good.

THE END

TO FOLLOW ANOTHER PATH, TURN TO PAGE 9.

You follow Big-ole Bayer as he pounds out of the alley and down the middle of a narrow street. As you catch up to him, you hear a gunshot, then a loud *whump* as Big-ole Bayer's body hits the ground.

No! you think, but you keep running. You duck behind a garbage truck as another shot shatters the air. After waiting for an hour, you sneak back out. Big-ole Bayer's body is gone, and so is whoever shot him. Retracing your steps to the manhole in the alley, you lower yourself into the sewer and run all the way back to the Bayer cottage.

41

TURN THE PAGE.

Wee Little and Medium are waiting for you. In tears, you report that Big-ole is dead, and the three of you weep together.

"We won't let this stop us," Wee Little finally says. "Right?"

"Right," you and Medium reply. You know that you have to fight harder than ever—for your mom, and also for Big-ole Bayer. You will never give up on bringing nature back to the World.

THE END

TO FOLLOW ANOTHER PATH, TURN TO PAGE 9.

You and Wee Little run, but before you get far, a hand grabs onto your shoulder and throws you against the wall of a hover-bike shop.

"I said hold it!" the voice whispers. He's got Wee Little by the paw.

You put your hands up. "What do you want?" you ask.

The flashlight lowers, and you see the face of a regular man—not a cop. "The cops went after the big guy. But I saw the whole thing. I saw you planting seeds."

"You are mistaken," Wee Little says.

TURN THE PAGE.

44

"Please, can I hold some?" the man says. "I just want to see what they feel like."

You and Wee Little exchange glances, then you open your bag. It's nearly empty after your night of planting, but the man reaches inside and pulls out a few seeds. "Beautiful," he says, staring. "Are they really real?"

"They're real," you say. "You can have them."

The man's eyes well with tears as he thanks you. "Listen, you better get out of here fast," he says. You shake hands and turn to run. But then you stop and say, "Water the plants, will you?" The man nods, and you smile. There are others like you. Others who want to experience nature. Maybe you really will change the World.

45

THE END

TO FOLLOW ANOTHER PATH, TURN TO PAGE 9.

Wee LITTLE BeaR

You're the oldest of three bear brothers. You're also the smallest, and you hate your name: Wee Little Bear. What kind of name is that? An embarrassing one, that's what kind.

Your youngest brother is the biggest—he's big in every sense of the word, except in the brain department. His name, naturally, is Big Bear. Your middle brother, Medium Bear, is a whiny worrywart. Keeping the two of them under control is a full-time job. Sometimes you get tired of being the responsible one.

47

For instance, Big Bear was in charge of getting food today, and he did a very poor job of it. He tried, but things don't always go so well for Big.

He got tangled up in the fishing net and fell in the water, letting all the fish get away. He gathered some berries but accidentally smashed them in his big, clumsy paws. Then he gathered mushrooms—but not the right kind—and nearly poisoned all three of you.

"Your name should be Big Dimwit," you mutter. You empty out the last of the grains from the bin and cook up some porridge. While it cools you go into the woods to search for nuts. But you don't find anything, and it doesn't take long for Medium to start whining, "I'm starving! Let's just eat the porridge plain." You give up and head home.

You reach the clearing where your cottage sits. You are surprised to see that the front door is slightly open. Cautiously the three of you creep up to the door and peek inside. Nobody is in sight. You step inside, and Big Bear lets out a terrible cry.

"Somebody has been eating my porridge!" he booms. About one spoonful has been taken from his giant bowl—big deal.

"Hey, somebody's been eating my porridge too," says Medium. He looks like he is about to cry even though his bowl is still nearly full.

But your bowl is totally empty. "Somebody has been eating mine too," you snarl. "And look! It's all gone." You look around. Someone's been here, but who?

TO SEARCH IN THE LIVING ROOM, TURN TO PAGE 50.

TO SEARCH UPSTAIRS, TURN TO PAGE 51.

Big Bear thunders into the living room, and you and Medium follow. "Hey!" Big says, seeing his cushion on the floor. "I think someone's been sitting in my chair!"

Medium Bear says, "Someone's been sitting in my chair too! The cushion is crooked!" Medium is very particular about his chair.

Neither of them notices that your chair is totally broken. It's a worthless pile of sticks. "Well, look at my chair!" you say.

Big starts sniffing the air and looking around. You sniff too. The intruder, whatever it is, is still in the house. Are you in danger? As the head of the household, you have to decide.

TO CONTINUE YOUR SEARCH UPSTAIRS, TURN TO PAGE 54.

TO SEEK SAFETY OUTSIDE THE HOUSE, TURN TO PAGE 56.

As the oldest, it's up to you to investigate. You see a dollop of porridge near the staircase and decide to search upstairs. At the top of the steps, you see a lump in your bed. A fan of pale hair lays across your pillow. You have heard that humans can grow out their hair—but you've never met one in real life. You wonder what other dangerous tricks they know.

A wrinkly hand pushes the covers away to reveal an old woman's face. You chuckle to yourself. How could she be dangerous?

"That's my bed," you tell her, not sure what else to say in this odd situation.

51

"Well that one was too hard," she says, pointing to Big's bed. Then she points to Medium's bed. "And that one was too soft. This one is just right."

TURN THE PAGE.

"I agree. But that doesn't explain what you're doing here," you say.

"I was waiting for you," she says. "But I got tired, so I took a nap."

"Why are you waiting for me?"

She holds out her hand, and you shake it. "I'm Goldilocks, and I have something to show you," she says, digging in a satchel. She pulls out a complicated wad of netting and begins to open it up. "No need for concern. Just be still, little guy."

"Big! Medium!" you yell, suddenly feeling very unsafe. "You better get up here!"

Your brothers come clomping up the stairs in time to see Goldilocks throw her net over your head.

"Hey!" Big says. "That's my brother. Let him go or … I'll eat you!" Medium looks at Big in horror then starts to bite his claws nervously.

TO TELL BIG BEAR TO EAT HER, **TURN TO PAGE 58.**

TO TELL MEDIUM BEAR TO CALL THE COPS, **TURN TO PAGE 60.**

Your brothers follow you upstairs. When you get to the landing, Big Bear points to his bed and scratches his head. "I think somebody's been sleeping in my bed," he says, looking at the wadded-up covers.

"Somebody's been sleeping in my bed," Medium whines, noticing a small wrinkle in his bedspread.

"Guess what, Einsteins?" you say. "Somebody's been sleeping in *my* bed—and still is."

An old woman springs up from your bed and exclaims, "Bears! Adorable bears!"

"And you are …?" you ask.

"Goldilocks." She points to the logo on her shirt: GOLDILOCKS ZOO. "I heard that there might be bears in this cottage. I've been looking for some really cute bears for my zoo, and you're the cutest I've ever seen! Guess I fell asleep waiting for you."

"We're not going to any zoo," you say, shaking your head.

"And we're not cute," Big Bear says, offended.

"Well, I'm sort of cute," Medium pouts.

"Yes, you are!" Goldilocks coos in a baby voice. Big Bear growls.

"Life in the zoo is a life of luxury!" Goldilocks continues. "We have a swimming pool and rocks to climb. And all the nuts and fish and honey you can eat! And you'll be famous! People will come from all over to see you! Come on, just give it a try. If you don't like it, I'll personally bring you back home." She smiles. "Promise."

"All-you-can-eat honey?" Big Bear says, drool 55 oozing from his muzzle. You think about the bowls of gloppy porridge on the table. Free food does sound pretty good.

TO GO WITH GOLDILOCKS TO CHECK OUT HER ZOO, TURN TO PAGE 62.

TO TELL HER NO THANKS, TURN TO PAGE 65.

Some bears might be too proud to abandon their house and hide in the woods, but not you. Better safe than sorry. You can't tell from the scent exactly what kind of intruder is in your house, but you don't think it's friendly. It's already eaten your food and broken your chair. What kind of monster is it?

"Let's burn down the cottage!" Big Bear says. "That'll get the intruder out!"

You look at him and shake your head. "Hello! Think it through, Big. Then we'd have no house." Big nods like he's trying to figure out a complicated math problem.

"What if the intruder is touching my teddy bears?" Medium moans.

Then you hear a noise like a creaking iron gate coming from upstairs. After a couple seconds, you realize it is someone yawning—loudly.

The three of you form a bear ladder to see inside the bedroom window. You peek in. "An old woman's in my bed!" you whisper.

Big starts laughing and your ladder collapses. "You were afraid of a little old lady!" Your face burns with embarrassment.

TO GO REMOVE THE WOMAN YOURSELF, TURN TO PAGE 66.

TO SET A TRAP TO LURE HER OUT, TURN TO PAGE 69.

"Go right ahead!" you say, fighting with the netting. "Eat her!"

Big Bear pumps his fist. "Yes!"

"No!" Goldilocks yells. She steps away from you, and you get a glimpse of what it says on her shirt: "GOLDILOCKS ZOO. Owner: Goldilocks." She wants to put you in a zoo!

Big clumsily tries to catch her. She runs behind the bed. Big chases her, but they just run in circles. Then Goldilocks grabs the blanket off your bed.

58   "This will be just right!" she says. She dashes for the open window and jumps out, using the blanket as a parachute and landing softly on the ground below. The three of you watch out the window as she scampers into the woods, quite nimbly for an old gal, you think.

"I almost had her!" Big Bear says, though he wasn't even close.

"Just look at this mess!" whines Medium.

"Help me out of this net!" you bark.

After freeing you, Big Bear asks, "So, what's a zoo?"

You know what a zoo is. And you hate to think of all those animals trapped by that mean, sneaky old Goldilocks.

TURN TO PAGE 71.

"Call the police!" you yell. "Tell them we have a kidnapping in progress!" Big and Medium bang down the stairs to get the phone. A few minutes later, having gotten you all tied up, Goldilocks is dragging you downstairs. You hear a knock at the door. Medium opens it, and standing on the step are two police officers—beavers with badges.

"All right, tell us what happened," one of the beavers asks, chewing on his pencil.

"Can't you see I'm being kidnapped?" you say from under the net.

Goldilocks holds out a badge of her own. "I own the zoo," she says coldly. "I am merely reclaiming an escaped bear." She gives the beavers a hard stare. "I hope I don't need to catch any escaped beavers," she threatens. The two beavers step back nervously.

"I'm not an escaped bear!" you yell.

The pencil-chewing beaver answers a call on his radio: "Roger that. We're done here. Heading back to the station." The beavers tip their hats and quickly scurry away, calling out, "Sorry, Wee Little. Lock your door next time!"

The old woman drags you out of the cottage. You watch over her shoulder as your brothers limply wave goodbye. You see Big Bear scratch his big, dumb head, trying to figure out what just happened. "So Wee Little wasn't really our brother?" he asks Medium.

Medium shrugs and calls after you, "Who's going to make our porridge now?" You shake your head in disgust. At least in the zoo you won't be responsible for these two anymore.

THE END

TO FOLLOW ANOTHER PATH, TURN TO PAGE 9.

You have to admit, you're curious about this zoo. Finding food every week is a pain, especially when it's Big's turn. It would not be such a bad thing to have food delivered to you every day.

The four of you hike through the woods to Goldilocks' big van. You're slightly concerned about the painting on the side showing a gorilla wearing a pink tutu. But you quickly forget about it when she hands you a big basket of berries to munch on during the ride. She drives you to the zoo and parks in a big garage. The van doors fling open and several men in white jumpsuits stand before you. Two of them hold stun guns.

"Look, our own personal bodyguards!" Big Bear says.

"I not so sure, big guy," you say. The hairs on the back of your neck stand up in alarm.

You follow Goldilocks to a big room decorated to look like a forest. As you walk in, you turn to ask a question, but the door slams behind you. She waves at you through a giant window.

"Hey!" you yell, pounding on the thick glass.

"Enjoy!" she mouths through the window. She walks away. You know she will never let you out.

TURN THE PAGE.

You look around the room and realize how small it is. When you go for a walk in the "woods," you have only 50 feet before you hit a wall and have to turn around. There's a stream running through a corner, but it's just an electric fountain trickling the same dribble of water through it over and over. No salmon leap out of that stream. And the trees are fake—no nuts, no berries.

"I'm hungry," Big Bear says. He heads over to barrel of what looks like dog food and digs in.

"I forgot my teddy bear!" Medium wails.

"We have bigger problems at the moment," you say. All around you, behind glass walls, stand human beings, laughing, pointing, and watching your every move.

THE END

TO FOLLOW ANOTHER PATH, TURN TO PAGE 9.

"We won't be going to any zoo today," you say.

"No?" she says. "Okay, fine. Your loss. I know lots of other bears who are dying to get in." She slings her bag over her shoulder then turns and says, "Say, have you heard about the big bad wolf that's been around? Would one of you mind walking me to my van so I don't get eaten?"

You don't know about any wolves in these parts, but you can't be too careful. You've heard terrible stories of wolves eating old ladies and then wearing their clothes. Maybe you should go with her.

65

TO SEND HER ON HER WAY, TURN TO PAGE 73.

TO WALK HER TO HER VAN, TURN TO PAGE 75.

You puff up your chest and stand tall—at least, as tall as you can. "I'll take care of this," you say.

"Make sure she doesn't sit in my chair again!" Medium Bear says.

You march inside and yell, "Hey, lady!"

The old woman walks down the stairs. "You're finally home! I've been waiting for you!" she says.

"Uh," you say, forgetting that you're supposed to be throwing her out.

"I'm from the Zookeeper's Clearinghouse. You and your brothers have won a fabulous prize!"

"Prize?"

"A free vacation in beautiful Goldilocks Zoo!" She unrolls a large poster that looks like a bank check. "Redeem for one free vacation!" it says.

"Vacation?" you say.

Curious to know what's going on, your brothers have come in. "What's a zoo?" Big asks.

"It's a resort for animals!" the woman says with excitement.

"With a swimming pool?" Medium asks.

"A swimming pool filled with honey!" she says.

You turn to see that Big has already pulled out his suitcase and is packing his favorite spoon. Medium heads upstairs, calling back, "Let me get my teddy bear!"

You stand with your hands on your hips. You're beginning to get an idea. "You go on ahead. I'll stay **67** here and take care of things until you get back."

TURN THE PAGE.

Big shrugs. "OK, Wee Little, but it's a once-in-a-lifetime opportunity."

Medium, coming back down with his teddy, says, "Don't let anyone sit in my chair while I'm gone."

You nod and wave while the woman herds Big and Medium out the door. "Sure you don't want to join us?" she asks with a twinkle in her eye.

"Nope, you go have fun," you say. You wave and close the door after them. You turn to look at the table. The first thing you do is dump the rest of Big's and Medium's porridge into your bowl. Then you sit down to eat it in Big's chair with your feet up on Medium's cushion. "Ah ... this is just right," you say with a smile on your face.

THE END

TO FOLLOW ANOTHER PATH, TURN TO PAGE 9.

"I have a plan," you say.

"You need a pan?" Big asks.

"No, a plan! Just do what I tell you!" Quietly, so as not to wake her, you spend the next hour building a trap. Finally you reach over the welcome mat and knock on the door. "Yoo-hoo!" you say. "Little old lady, please come out!"

She opens the door and steps out, which triggers a pail of flowers above to tip onto her head. The welcome mat she steps on has a skateboard underneath it, which begins to roll forward until she hits a rope stretched across the sidewalk, tripping her. She flies forward and lands on the up-end of a teeter-totter, bringing it down and sending the other end up, which launches a soccer ball into the air, which knocks into a beehive.

TURN THE PAGE.

The bees pour out of the hive and race toward the old lady, who is covered in flowers. She runs

screaming into the woods, followed by the bees.

"Just as I planned," you say and stick your hand inside the hive, which is now bee free. You and your brothers eat all the honey without a single sting.

THE END

TO FOLLOW ANOTHER PATH, TURN TO PAGE 9.

You and your brothers trail Goldilocks to the Goldilocks Zoo and hide in some bushes at the edge of the parking lot. At the end of the day, after the cars clear out, you walk up to the main gates. They're locked.

"Big, open it up," you say, and your brother raises a gigantic hind paw and kicks the gate open. Chunks of metal fly. The three of you walk into the zoo's plaza and look around. There's a snack bar nearby, and Big Bear rips open the door and helps himself to nachos.

"Let's go!" you hiss at him. He takes a tray with him as you go around the zoo. You are outraged to see so many animals behind bars. You set Big to work breaking open all the cages.

"Come on out!" you call as each animal is sprung free.

TURN THE PAGE.

Big rips down fences so the lions and tigers can escape. You find keys and unlock all the reptiles. Soon snakes, lizards, geckos, and turtles are crawling about. You unlock the polar bear exhibit, but the polar bear stays put. "No thanks. Too warm out there," he says.

It is late at night by the time you've freed all the animals, and you are tired as you walk toward home. You have gained a few friends—a panther, a parrot, and a monkey.

"I'm hungry," Big Bear says.

"I'm hungry," mocks the parrot. Medium Bear, the panther, and the monkey all agree.

You realize you're hungry too. And now you have more mouths to feed. "Do you guys like porridge?" you ask.

THE END

TO FOLLOW ANOTHER PATH, TURN TO PAGE 9.

"Sorry lady. You're on your own," you say. Better safe than sorry. She could be trying to trick you.

After she's gone, you see that she left a net behind. *Aha!* You think. Clearly she had been planning to capture you!

You and Medium decide to go fishing with Goldilocks' net. But Big Bear stays behind, claiming he needs a nap. You and Medium head to the stream. The net is perfect for the job, and you catch three nice, big salmon. One for each of you.

"Dinnertime!" you call out to Big when you get home. But there's no answer. You and Medium eat your salmon, wondering where Big has gone. Finally he comes through the door and collapses into his extra large chair, not even glancing at the salmon. His belly is swollen to a massive size.

TURN THE PAGE.

"You didn't," you say.

"Maybe I did," Big says with a satisfied smile.

"You ate her?"

"He ate Goldilocks?" Medium asks. "Oh, you'll get terrible heartburn, Big!"

Big Bear burps. "Sorry," he says. "I was so hungry. And she smelled like nutmeg," he adds dreamily.

You sigh. And here you were worried about a wolf getting her. "Well, how was she?" you ask.

74 "At first I thought she was too stringy," Big says. "Then I thought she was too dense. Turns out, she was just right."

THE END

TO FOLLOW ANOTHER PATH, TURN TO PAGE 9.

You volunteer to walk Goldilocks to her van. As you approach, a howl comes from the woods. "The wolf!" Goldilocks squeals. "Quick—get in the van! We'll be safe there." Better safe than sorry, you think. You hop into the back of the van and Goldilocks slams the door behind you. The lock clicks. Then the howl dissolves into laughter. "Nice job," Goldilocks says. You look out the small window and see her laughing with another woman. They both have GOLDILOCKS ZOO on their shirts. You've been trapped.

My brothers will rescue me, you think. Then you picture your big, dim-witted brother and your worrying middle brother. Big will never even figure out where you are, much less how to get you out. And Medium will be too scared to even try. You're doomed.

75

THE END

TO FOLLOW ANOTHER PATH, TURN TO PAGE 9.

CHAPTER 4

ALL THE ANSWERS IN THE PALM OF YOUR HAND

Ever since you got your awesome new smartphone, the Goldilocks9000, you never leave home without it. In fact you hardly do anything without it. Today your mom got mad at you for constantly being on your phone. "You never do anything real!" she said. "I'm worried you have RDD—Real-Life Deficit Disorder. Why don't you go play in the woods?"

"Okay," you told her. Of course you brought your phone with you.

77

You look at the weather app on your phone. It predicts a sunny afternoon. You check the MapMyWoods app to find a good path to hike on. You post a selfie on your favorite social network, FairyTalesagram. Finally you walk into the woods, still eyeing the screen. A weird shape appears on it. It's round and blurry. You realize it's a raindrop.

You look up and see dark clouds above. Then it begins to pour. Stupid weather app. You run along the path, but you become lost and soaked. After a while you come across a little house in the clearing. Without a second thought, you go inside, desperate to keep your phone safe and dry.

You stand dripping wet and shivering inside the small cottage. As you shake the water droplets off your phone, you can't help but notice three bowls of porridge on the table. You're so hungry you just have to try it.

You take a seat in front of the big bowl. But the porridge is much too hot, and besides that, the chair is much too hard. You move over to the medium bowl and sit. This chair is too soft and you sink into it, hitting your chin on your knees. And this porridge is too cold. The small bowl and chair, though, are just right. But as you take the last bite of porridge, you hear the chair creak. A second later it collapses and you find yourself on the floor.

You panic—you don't want to get in trouble! You're not sure what breaking and entering is, but you just entered something and broke something, so you're probably guilty of it. But you're also still sopping wet and want to get your phone dried off before it's ruined.

TO LOOK UP INSTRUCTIONS ON YOUR SMARTPHONE TO FIX THE CHAIR, **TURN TO PAGE 80.**

TO GO UPSTAIRS TO LOOK FOR A TOWEL, **TURN TO PAGE 81.**

You better try to fix the chair. You check the label and see that it's made by a furniture company called Twigs R Us! You go online and easily find the instructions. But the instructions are in words. Whoever heard of written instructions? Pictures—you need pictures and interactive diagrams!

You look outside and see that the rain is dying down, so you decide to leave before you cause more trouble. But at that moment you hear voices outside. It must be the people who live here. Uh-oh. How would your mom feel about the "real-life" experience of going to jail for trespassing in someone's house? Not good. You could run upstairs to hide. Or you could try talking to them. Maybe they would be understanding about all this.

TO RUN UPSTAIRS, TURN TO PAGE 84.

TO FACE THEM, TURN TO PAGE 86.

Your wet clothes stick to your body as you reach the top of the stairs and look around. Three beds are arranged against one wall, and three towels hang on another. You grab a towel and begin scrubbing your hair. You can't help but notice that the towel smells a bit … gamey.

You look out the window and see that it has stopped raining. The beautiful day that the weather app promised might happen after all. Just as you're about to head downstairs to get out of there, your phone vibrates. Your friend Jack posted on FairyTalesagram: "About to climb this huge beanstalk! #adventure." Jack is always bragging about his adventures.

TURN THE PAGE.

You decide to brag about your own adventure, so you climb on one of the beds and start jumping, taking selfies in midair. You do splits and flips. You send an awesome upside-down shot to Jack: "Jumping on a stranger's bed in a scary house in the woods! #trueadventure."

You hit send and lie back to catch your breath. You're worn out from all that jumping. While you're lying there, you begin to play a new game on your phone that you didn't even realize you had. It's called Angry Bears. In it three bears try to figure out who is sleeping in their bed.

Uh-oh. You bolt awake. This is not a game. You fell asleep and started dreaming! Through a tiny slit in your eye, you see three real bears staring at you—a papa, a mama, and a baby.

You wonder if you can run to the window and jump out before the big, beefy bears can react. But you've also heard that bears will leave you alone if you play dead.

TO JUMP OUT THE WINDOW, TURN TO PAGE 87.

TO PLAY DEAD, TURN TO PAGE 88.

You scramble up the stairs just before the front door opens. You tiptoe quietly to the edge of the landing and look down. It's three bears!

You crawl away from the landing and try to squeeze under one of the three beds to hide, but it's too low and you can't fit. You try the next bed, but it's so high you're not hidden at all. You try the third bed, and it's just right for hiding.

Meanwhile you hear the three bears downstairs, talking about the porridge. The littlest bear is upset that somebody ate all of his porridge. Then they notice the chairs. "Somebody's been sitting in my chair!" says a deep voice. "Somebody's been sitting in my chair too!" moans a softer voice. "Somebody's been sitting in my chair, and it's busted!" whines a small, baby voice.

You open up the web browser on your phone and are about to research bear behavior when you hear heavy footsteps clomping up the stairs. Maybe you can learn something about how to make friends with bears after you've broken into their house. The web has answers about everything. On the other hand, maybe you should try to escape. You just noticed an open window you could probably climb out of it.

TO RESEARCH ABOUT BEARS, TURN TO PAGE 91.

TO CLIMB OUT THE WINDOW, TURN TO PAGE 93.

You stand up and wait for the door to open. When it does, you're stunned to see a big, strong, papa bear followed by a slightly smaller mama bear. Bringing up the rear is a cute little baby bear.

"Hi!" you say. "Don't worry, I won't hurt you!" That seems like a ridiculous thing to say to bears, but it's all you can think of.

The baby bear points to his bowl. "Somebody has been eating my porridge," he says. "And it's all gone!"

The three bears look at you. They don't look happy. When they notice the broken chair at your feet, they look even less happy. "I bet I know who ate the porridge," the papa bear says. "And I bet I know who broke that chair."

"I can explain," you say.

TO INVENT A LIE FOR WHY YOU'RE THERE, TURN TO PAGE 96.

TO TELL THEM THE TRUTH AND APOLOGIZE, TURN TO PAGE 98.

"Ahhhhh!" With a crazy yell, you rush toward the window and dive out headfirst. You flip in the air to land on your feet, but one foot rolls sideways with a disturbing *crack*. You collapse in horrible pain.

All three bears peer at you out the window. "Who was dat?" the little one asks.

You're hurt and scared, but old habits die hard. So you take out your Goldilocks9000 to snap a selfie with the bears in the background. (Jack will sure be impressed!)

You don't have time to think about that now, though, because the bears are headed your way. They seem more curious than angry. Maybe they'd be willing to help you? Or maybe you shouldn't risk it and should run.

TO WAIT AND ASK THEM FOR HELP, TURN TO PAGE 99.

TO RUN INTO THE WOODS, TURN TO PAGE 101.

You play dead, hoping it will work. You keep your eyes closed and wait. The baby bear says, "Someone has been sleeping in my bed, and that someone is still there!"

The bears sniff you all over, from your toes to your ears. It tickles like crazy, but you don't move a muscle. It takes everything you have not to scream and run away.

"Well, it looks like this human just crawled in your bed and died," the mama says. "How do these pests keep getting in?"

TURN THE PAGE.

"Eww—it's dead?" asks the baby bear. "But look! It left behind the new Goldilocks9000." You hear him pick up your phone and start to play with it.

"Cool!" says the papa bear. "Let me see."

"I found it—it's mine!" Baby Bear replies. You hear them scuffling next to the bed. You open your eyes just a crack and see them wrestling on the floor.

Mama Bear yells, "Stop bickering and just help me get this body out of here!"

The bears carry you downstairs and into the woods. "The wolves will eat it tonight," you hear one say as they walk away.

You wait until you can't hear them before opening your eyes. You really want your phone back. Would it be crazy to sneak back and try to get it?

TO TRY TO FIND YOUR WAY HOME, TURN TO PAGE 103.

TO GO BACK AND TRY TO GET YOUR PHONE, TURN TO PAGE 104.

You quickly type "how to make bears like you" into your search engine. But your fingers stumble and it auto-corrects to "how to mail bears thank yous." Drat!

The bears are coming upstairs. The biggest one lumbers over, reaches a paw under the bed where you're hiding, and yanks you out. You scream like a hyena, and the bears jump back in surprise. You take the opportunity to bound down the stairs two at a time, out the door, and into the woods.

When you finally stop to get your bearings, you don't recognize anything. It's all trees and bushes. Luckily you have the convenient MapMyWoods app. You reach into your pocket, but ... no Goldilocks9000. You pat your other pockets, but it's not there either. You must have dropped it during your escape.

TURN THE PAGE.

Panic sets in. How will you get home now? You look around. The sun is setting to your right, which is west. You remember that you walked east when you left home, so now you should walk west, toward the sunset. *Hey, I figured that out without my phone compass!* you think. To your surprise you make your way through the woods and finally home.

You're sitting in your room feeling pretty proud of yourself when your mom comes in. "Quick," she says. "Get out your phone and find us a roofer on that Findaworker app. We've got a bad leak."

At first you don't move. You're about to admit that you lost your phone when you get another idea. "Maybe I can fix the roof," you say. "Sounds like good real-life experience, don't you think?"

92

THE END

TO FOLLOW ANOTHER PATH, TURN TO PAGE 9.

Quickly, before the bears reach the bedroom, you climb out the window. Holding onto the windowsill, you lower your feet, then let go and drop to the ground. You tuck into a roll to cushion your fall. (You learned how to fall safely by playing Escape the Stampeding Elephants on your phone.)

You run into the woods, relieved. Whistling a happy tune, you wander along the path. It doesn't take long to get totally lost, but you're not worried. You'll just fire up the MapMyWoods app and let it show you the way home. You push buttons over and over but you can't get a signal. When you finally reach a path that you recognize, you get excited. Night has fallen, but this area looks sort of familiar. Maybe you've been trick or treating here before?

TURN THE PAGE.

You approach a clearing and see a house with a light burning inside. Maybe they'll give you directions.

A large bear answers the door. You realize you have walked in a circle and arrived back at the same house.

"I'm lost," you manage to whisper.

"Oh, you must be cold and hungry," the bear says. "Come in. Dinner's ready."

As you nervously step inside, he turns to you. "How do you like your porridge—hot or cold?" He puts a paw on your shoulder and winks. "I bet you like it somewhere in between."

A shiver runs up your spine as you sit at the
table with the three bears. Soon Baby Bear begins
to sniff the air around you curiously. He looks
at you then looks over at his broken chair and
narrows his eyes accusingly.

Now you're busted.

THE END

TO FOLLOW ANOTHER PATH, TURN TO PAGE 9.

You show them your smartphone. "I have an app on here that detects when criminals are nearby. And I ... tracked one to your house! But ... he must have escaped as soon as I walked in."

The mama bear turns to the papa. "I told you your brother was in town again."

"Now, you don't know it was Lyle ..." Papa says.

"I'm sorry I couldn't be more of a help," you say, backing out while secretly snapping pictures with your phone. You want proof of this crazy adventure.

But as you're inching toward the door, the baby bear pipes up. "Oh, can we keep it?" he asks. "I've always wanted a human!"

"Absolutely not," Papa says.

"I'll take real good care of it, Papa. I promise!"

"Oh, let him keep the human," the mama bear says. "He's wanted one for so long. And it sounds like this one might help keep burglars away."

Papa Bear lets out a sigh. "All right," he says. "But the first time I have to clean up after him, we're taking him to the pound."

Baby Bear jumps up and down. "Yay!" He runs over and hugs you. "Come on, I'll show you my room."

That night you find yourself pinned under Baby Bear's arms as he goes "night-night." You wonder if the Goldilocks9000 can get you out of this one.

THE END

TO FOLLOW ANOTHER PATH, TURN TO PAGE 9.

"I'm sorry," you say. "It was me. I ate the porridge. I was so hungry. And I broke the chair, but I didn't mean to." You hang your head in shame. They look at you for a few seconds, and you notice their sharp claws and long teeth. You hope they forgive you, because if they don't, you're in trouble.

Finally the papa bear opens the door. "Get!" he yells at you. "Go on, get out! Shoo!"

"But before you go," Mama Bear cuts in, "we'll take that fancy phone as payment for the damages."

She reaches out her big meaty paw. Reluctantly you hand over the Goldilocks9000. You decide that giving it up will help you with your Real-Life Deficit Disorder. Not to mention that if you don't give it to her, you'll be at risk of a No-Life Disorder.

98

THE END

TO FOLLOW ANOTHER PATH, TURN TO PAGE 9.

The three bears come out of the house toward you, and you wave in what you hope is a friendly looking way.

"Hi!" you say. "I was wondering if you could help me find my way home. I'm lost."

The bears come up and start sniffing you. The big one licks your arm.

"What is it?" asks the baby bear.

"It's a human," grunts the papa.

"I've never had human," the mama says. "Shall we try it?"

"What do you mean, 'try it'?" you ask.

Baby Bear nods his head. "Yeah, since my porridge is all gone."

99

TURN THE PAGE.

"Whatever my boy wants," Papa Bear says, pinching the little one's cheek.

"I'll go start the soup pot," Mama Bear says, turning toward the house.

You try to get up and run, but your ankle won't hold you. You collapse again. You try to call your mom on your phone, but Papa Bear takes it away before you can press send. "Nice! The Goldilocks9000," he says, admiring it. "I bet we can find a good recipe online."

"Hey, that's mine!" you say as he slings you over his shoulder. "Can I just see if I got any 'likes' on FairyTalesagram?"

But the bear's not listening. He's busy typing "human soup recipe" into the search engine.

THE END

TO FOLLOW ANOTHER PATH, TURN TO PAGE 9.

You pick up your phone and hop into the woods, unable to put any weight on your foot. You glance back to see the bears watching you with confused expressions. They're probably thinking you're some odd species of rabbit. Once in the woods, you crouch in the bushes, listening for the bears. But they never come.

After an hour you crawl back onto the path and look around. There's no sign of the bears. You try to step on your foot, but you can't. Your ankle must be broken. You pull out your phone. The screen is cracked, but you are able to do a search for how to treat a broken ankle: "Use something hard and flat to set a splint," it says.

101

TURN THE PAGE.

You know what you have to do. Wincing with
pain, you tear a sleeve from your sweatshirt and
wrap your hard, flat phone tightly against your
ankle. Carefully, you stand up. It still hurts like
crazy, but at least you can walk on it. Keeping as
much weight off your phone-foot as possible, you
limp toward home, wondering what's wrong with
a little Real-Life Deficit Disorder.

102

THE END

TO FOLLOW ANOTHER PATH, TURN TO PAGE 9.

Who cares about the phone? You escaped death once—you can't risk it again. You run down the path but you get tired. You think maybe you should be exercising more instead of playing games on your phone.

You walk for a couple hours, lost without your map app. Finally you come to a house that seems to be made of cake and candy. Maybe you can get directions. As you approach, the front door opens. An old woman with a big nose smiles and holds out her hand. In her long, bony fingers is a beautiful smartphone you've never seen before.

"Would you like to see the Gingerbread 2.0? Best phone on the market!" she cackles. Though she seems a little strange, you step inside. You can't wait to check out that phone.

103

THE END

TO FOLLOW ANOTHER PATH, TURN TO PAGE 9.

You aren't going anywhere without your phone. You wait until nightfall, then sneak back to the bears' house and peek in the window. You see the three of them gathered at the table with your phone. "Look at that one!" Mama Bear says, and they all laugh.

They're looking at your FairyTalesagram photos. That means they've seen all your selfies. They know you were jumping on their beds.

Your phone rings, and Papa Bear answers it. "Hello?" He listens for a second, the phone looking tiny in his huge paw. "I'm sorry. That person is ... no longer with us." He chuckles as he hangs up and says to the other bears, "It was the human's mother. Humans are so careless with their offspring!"

Your mother! She must be worried sick.
You've got to get back home. You remember what
the bears said about the wolves, so you don't dare
stop to rest. You start walking, but you can't see
a thing in the dark. Without your flashlight app,
your map app, and all your other apps, you
fear you'll never make it home.

THE END

TO FOLLOW ANOTHER PATH, TURN TO PAGE 9.

THREE BEARS AND A FOX WHO BECAME GOLDILOCKS

The history of *Goldilocks and the Three Bears* begins with a story that did not have a golden-haired girl named Goldilocks. Long before that little girl came along, and before any version of the story was written down, people in England told a tale called "Scrapefoot."

107

This story features a fox named Scrapefoot as the character who enters the home of three bears. He is afraid of the bears but is curious to learn about them.

Instead of porridge, the fox drinks milk. When the bears catch him in their home, they debate about how to kill him. Finally they throw him out the upstairs window. But Scrapefoot lands unhurt and runs into the woods.

A woman named Eleanor Mure wrote and illustrated the story as a gift for her nephew in 1831. In her story the fox is changed to a cranky old woman. When the bears catch her, they try to kill her first by burning, then by drowning. When these methods don't work, they impale her on a church steeple!

Robert Southey was the first to publish the story. Southey was also the first to change the milk to porridge. His old woman, like Mure's, is described as mean, nasty, and rude. At the end of Southey's story, the old woman escapes by jumping out the window and running away.

Then in 1849 a writer named Joseph Cundall published his own version of the story, the first one in which the home invader is a young girl. Her name was "Silver Hair." Nine years after that, the tale was collected in *Aunt Mavor's Nursery Tales*, with the girl now being called "Silver-Locks." In 1868 when the story appeared in *Aunt Friendly's Nursery Book*, her name became "Golden Hair." She finally became "Goldilocks" in 1904, when the story was collected in *Old Nursery Stories and Rhymes*.

The bears have changed over the years too. In Southey's version they were all male: Little, Small, Wee Bear; Middle-sized Bear; and Great, Huge Bear. A later version had the two larger bears being brother and sister, with the smallest being their friend. Around 1860 they became a Father, Mother, and Baby Bear.

In the version we're familiar with today, the bears are a family and the cute little girl escapes unharmed. This story is nowhere near as frightening as the older versions that featured murderous bears and an evil old woman.

This long-standing tale is famous as a beloved bedtime story, in fairy tale books, and even on screen. One of the more enduring versions was made in 1944 when Warner Brothers made a Looney Tunes cartoon. In it Bugs Bunny starred as Goldilocks.

CRITICAL THINKING
USING THE COMMON CORE

✧ This book offers three new versions of the Goldilocks story. In Chapter 3 Goldilocks plays a villain. What is a villain? Think about the traditional Goldilocks story you know. Does that version have a villain? (Craft and Structure)

✧ In Chapter 5 the author tells about the different versions of the Goldilocks story throughout history. Describe in your own words how the story changed over the years. (Key Ideas and Details)

✧ Imagine your own Goldilocks story. What is the setting? How would the characters and plot be different from the traditional tale? Would your version have a villain? (Integration of Knowledge and Ideas)

READ MORE

Bradman, Tony. *Goldilocks and the Just Right Club.* North Mankato: Stone Arch Books, 2009.

Calonita, Jen. *Flunked.* Fairy Tale Reform School. Naperville, Ill.: Sourcebooks Jabberwocky, 2015.

Doherty, Berlie. *Classic Fairy Tales: Candlewick Illustrated Classic.* Somerville, Mass.: Candlewick Press, 2009.

INTERNET SITES

Use FactHound to find Internet sites related to this book. All of the sites on FactHound have been researched by our staff.

Here's all you do:

Visit *www.facthound.com*

Type in this code: 9781491458556